GULLIVER'S TRAVELS

GULLIVER'S TRAVELS
By Jonathan Swift

Adapted by Kathleen Thompson
Illustrated by Yoshi Miyake

RSVP
RAINTREE
STECK-VAUGHN
P U B L I S H E R S
The Steck-Vaughn Company

Austin, Texas

Library of Congress Number: 88-27463

Library of Congress Cataloging-in-Publication Data

Thompson, Kathleen.
  Gulliver's travels / [adapted by] Kathleen Thompson; illustrated by Yoshi Miyake.

  Summary: The voyages of an Englishman carry him to such strange places as Lilliput, where people are six inches tall; Brobdingnag, a land of giants; an island of sorcerers; and a country ruled by horses.
  [1. Fantasy.] I. Thompson, Kathleen. II. Miyake, Yoshi, ill. III. Swift, Jonathan, 1667-1745. Gulliver's travels. IV. Title.
PZ7.G4817Gu [Fic.]-dc19   1988   88-27463

ISBN 0-8172-2763-6 hardcover library binding

ISBN 0-8114-6824-0 softcover binding

10 11   99 98

CONTENTS

A Voyage to Lilliput
CHAPTER ONE

My father had a small estate in Nottinghamshire. I was the third of five sons. And so, though he gave me what help he could, I had my own way to make in the world.

I was ship's doctor on a passage to the East Indies in 1699, when my ship was driven by a violent storm onto a rock. We were immediately split. Six of the crew, of whom I was one, let down a lifeboat into the sea. In about half an hour the boat was overturned by another storm from the north. What became of my companions in the boat I cannot tell. I swam as luck directed me.

When I was almost gone and able to struggle no longer, I found myself in shallow water. I walked forward near half a mile, but could not discover any sign of houses or people. I was extremely tired and I lay down on the grass, which was very short and soft. I slept sounder than I ever remember to have done in my life.

When I awaked, it was just daylight. I tried to rise, but was not able to stir. My arms and legs were strongly fastened on each side to the ground. My hair, which was long and thick, was tied down in the same manner. I could see nothing except the sky. In a little time I felt something alive moving on my left leg. Bending my eyes downward as much as I could, I saw it was a human creature not six inches high!

Soon I felt at least forty more of the same kind following the first. I was amazed, and roared so loud that they all ran back in a fright. However, they soon returned. Finally, struggling to get loose, I had the luck to break the strings

that fastened my left arm to the ground. At the same time, with a violent pull, which gave me great pain, I loosened the strings that tied down my hair on the left side so that I was just able to turn my head about two inches. In an instant, I felt more than a hundred arrows on my left hand, which pricked me like so many needles. I thought it best to lie still.

When the people saw I was quiet, they shot no more arrows. But I heard a knocking for more than an hour, like people at work. When I turned my head a little that way, I saw they had built a stage. One of the people stood on it and made a long speech. He acted the part of a great speaker. I did not understand a word of it, but I could see threats and promises, pity, and kindness.

I answered in a few words, most humbly. I put my finger on my mouth to show that I wanted food. He understood me very well. He commanded that several ladders should be set against my sides. Then, more than a hundred of the people climbed up and walked towards my mouth with baskets full of meat. I ate them by two or three at a mouthful, and took three loaves of bread at a time. Then they brought up one of their largest barrels. I drank it off. It held about half a pint and tasted like a Burgundy wine, but much more delicious.

I now thought myself bound by the laws of hospitality to a people who had treated me with so much expense and magnificence. And I wondered at the fearlessness of these tiny people who dared to climb and walk upon my body.

Soon I slept about eight hours, and it was no wonder, for the doctors, by the Emperor's order, had put a sleeping potion in the wine. It seems that upon the first moment I was discovered, the Emperor ordered a machine built to carry me to the capital city. Five hundred carpenters and engineers immediately set to work. Nine hundred of the strongest men raised and placed me on this vehicle. All this I was told, for the whole time I lay in a deep sleep. Fifteen hundred of the Emperor's largest horses were used to pull me towards the city.

At the place where we stopped, there was a building that had once been a temple. This was to be my home. The great gate in the front was about four foot high and almost two foot wide. I could easily creep through it. At this time, ninety chains, like those that hang to a lady's watch in Europe and almost as large, were locked to my left leg with six and thirty padlocks.

When the workmen decided it was impossible for me to break loose from the chains, they cut all the strings that bound me. The noise and amazement of the people at seeing me rise and walk are not to be expressed.

The country round looked like a garden, the fields like so many beds of flowers. The tallest trees seemed to be seven foot high. I saw the town on my left hand, which looked like the painted scene of a city in a theater.

The Emperor was there and looked me over with great wonder but kept beyond the length of my chains. He is taller by almost the width of my nail than any of his court, which alone is enough to strike an awe into those who see him. His clothes were very plain and simple, but he had on his head a light helmet of gold. He held his sword in his hand in case I should happen to break loose. It was almost three inches long and was decorated with diamonds.

The ladies and courtiers were all most magnificently dressed. The spot they stood on looked like a petticoat spread on the ground, embroidered with figures of gold and silver.

His Imperial Majesty spoke often to me, and I returned answers, but neither of us could understand a word. After about two hours, the court went away and left a strong guard to protect me. I was to need it. Some of the people of the country shot arrows at me, one of which barely missed my left eye.

The colonel of the guard ordered six of the ringleaders to be taken, and thought it proper to punish them by putting them, tied, into my hands. I took them all, put

five of them in my coat pocket, and made a face as though I was going to eat the sixth alive. The poor man squealed terribly, especially when I took out my penknife. But I cut his strings and set him gently on the ground, and away he ran. Then I treated the rest in the same way, taking them one by one out of my pocket. And I saw that the soldiers and people were grateful for my mercy.

The court had many difficulties about me. They feared that my diet would be very expensive and might cause a famine. Sometimes they decided to starve or to shoot me with poisoned arrows. But they feared the odor from my dead body might cause a plague in the kingdom. While they were thinking what to do with me, several officers of the army told of my behavior to the six criminals. They thought so well of this that, instead of killing me, the court ordered many things for my comfort.

All the villages near the city were ordered to deliver every morning six cows, forty sheep, and a quantity of bread and wine. His Majesty would pay for them from his treasury. Six hundred persons were hired to be my servants. It was ordered that three hundred tailors should make me a suit of clothes in the style of the country. Six of his Majesty's greatest scholars were sent to teach me their language.

In about three weeks, I had made great progress in learning their language. The Emperor frequently honored me with his visits. We spoke together, and the first words I learned expressed my desire that he would please give me my liberty. Every day I repeated this on my knees.

His answer was that this must be a work of time, and that first I must *Lumos kelmin pesso dessmar lon emposo* —swear a peace with him and his kingdom. Then the Emperor called for my sword, which I took out.

Immediately all the troops gave a shout between terror and surprise. The sun shone clear and the reflection dazzled their eyes as I waved the sword to and fro in my hand. Then his Majesty ordered me to cast it on the ground as gently as I could, about six foot from the end of my chain. Then he demanded one of the hollow iron pillars, by which he meant my pistols. I drew it out and, as well as I could, explained to him the use of it. Then, charging it only with powder, I let it off in the air.

Hundreds fell down as if they had been struck dead! Even the Emperor, although he stood his ground, could not recover himself for some time. I gave up my pistol in the same way as I had my sword. Then I handed over the contents of all my pockets, which the Emperor promised should be returned when I left. But there was one pocket I did not empty. In it were a pair of glasses, a pocket telescope, and a few other small things that could not be important to the Emperor but were to me. And I was afraid they might be lost or broken if I gave them over.

For some time I watched the life of the country — their work and their play. All the while, my gentleness and good nature gained so far with the Emperor and his court that I began to have hopes of my liberty. At last the day came that the court agreed to remove the chains from my leg. In return, I agreed to certain conditions. I have made a translation of these conditions as they were written down.

"First, The Man Mountain shall not leave our kingdom without our permission under our great seal.

"Secondly, He shall not come into our city unless we make a special arrangement, at which time the people shall have two hours' warning to keep within their doors.

"Thirdly, The Man Mountain shall, on his walks, keep to our main roads and not offer to walk or lie down in a meadow or field of corn.

"Fourthly, As he walks the roads, he shall take care not to trample upon the bodies of any of our loving subjects, their horses, or carriages; nor take any of our subjects into his hands without asking.

"Fifthly, He shall fight with us against our enemies in the Island of Blefuscu.

"Sixthly, He shall aid and assist our workmen in raising certain great stones.

"Lastly, The Man Mountain shall have a daily allowance of meat and drink that is enough for 1728 of our subjects."

I swore to these conditions with great cheerfulness and my chains were immediately unlocked.

CHAPTER TWO

One morning, about two weeks after I had been given my liberty, one of the kings advisers, Reldresal, came to my house.

"For more than seventy moons past," he said, "there have been two parties in this kingdom, under the names of *Tramecksan* — those who wear high heels on their shoes — and *Slamecksan* — those who wear low heels. These two parties will neither eat nor drink nor talk with each other. His Majesty uses only Low-Heels in the government, as you have probably noticed. But the prince, his son, seems to have some liking for the High-Heels. At least, we can plainly discover one of his heels higher than the other, which makes him walk strangely.

"Now, while this struggle is going on, we are facing a war with the Island of Blefuscu, which is the other great empire of the universe. (As to what you have said, that there are other kingdoms in the world where the people are as large as you, we prefer to think that you dropped from the moon or one of the stars. Because it is certain that even a hundred humans of your size would quickly destroy our kingdom.)

"The two great empires of Lilliput and Blefuscu have long been at war because of eggs. Everyone agrees that the old way of breaking boiled eggs before we eat them was upon the larger end. But his Majesty's grandfather, while he was a boy, broke an egg on the larger end and cut one of his fingers. Whereupon the Emperor his father commanded all his subjects to break the smaller end of their eggs.

"The people so hated this law that they six times waged war against their own Emperor. They were encouraged in this by the king of Blefuscu. And when each war ended, the rebels ran away to that empire. According to our figures, more than eleven thousand people have died rather than break their eggs at the smaller end.

"The Big-Endians who have run away to Blefuscu are the ones who started the war between that empire and this one. And now they have a large fleet of ships and are getting ready to invade us. The Emperor, who has great confidence in your strength and courage, has asked me to tell you of these things."

I asked Reldresal to let the Emperor know that, while I didn't want to get mixed up in party politics, I was ready to risk my life to defend him and his country.

The Empire of Blefuscu is separated from Lilliput only by a band of water eight hundred yards wide. The most experienced seamen told me that in the middle at high water it was seventy *glumguffs* deep, which is about six foot of European measure, and the rest of it is fifty *glumguffs* at most. Based on this information, I had an idea for taking the enemy's entire fleet.

First I asked for a great deal of the strongest rope and bars of iron. I tripled the rope to make it stronger. For the same reason, I twisted together three of the iron bars, which were about the size of knitting needles. I then bent the ends of the bars into hooks and attached the bars to the ropes.

I carried these to the coast where, putting off my shoes and stockings and my coat, I waded into the sea. I arrived at the enemy's fleet in less than half an hour.

The enemy was so frightened when they saw me that they leaped out of their ships and swam to shore. I then fastened one of my hooks to each ship and tied all the cords together. While I was doing this, the enemy shot several thousand arrows, which smarted greatly and disturbed my work. My greatest fear was for mine eyes. But I took out my glasses and fastened them as strongly

as I could upon my nose.

I now cut the anchor ropes of the ships with my pocketknife. Then I took up the ends of the ropes to which hooks were tied, and with great ease drew fifty of the enemy's largest battleships after me. I waded back across the channel and arrived safe at the royal port of Lilliput. There I cried out in a loud voice, "Long live the Emperor of Lilliput!" This great ruler received me with all possible praise and created me a *Nardac* upon the spot, which is the highest title of honor among them.

But then his Majesty wished me to help him completely overcome the Blefuscu people. I said that I would never help to bring a free and brave people into slavery. His Imperial Majesty could not forgive me for this. And when I asked his permission to travel to Blefuscu, he gave it to me in a very cold manner.

Some weeks after a treaty of peace was signed between the two countries, I was able to do the Emperor an excellent service. At least, I thought it was that at the time. I was awakened one midnight by the cries of many hundreds of people at my door. They begged me to come at once to the palace, where her Imperial Majesty's apartment was on fire. It had been started by the carelessness of a maid of honor, who fell asleep while she was reading a romantic novel.

As orders were given to clear the way before me — and it was a moonshine night — I got to the palace without trampling on any of the people. Once there I saw that the water was far away and the fire violent. The case seemed hopeless and the palace would certainly have burned to the ground if I had not suddenly thought of an idea.

I had not yet that morning emptied my water. This I now did in such a quantity, and in the proper places, that in three minutes the fire was entirely put out. And the rest of that noble palace, which had cost so many ages to build, was saved.

I later discovered that making water in the area around the palace was against the law and could be punished by death. And the Empress, hating what I had done, swore that the buildings should never be repaired for her use and also that she would have her revenge on me.

CHAPTER THREE

Here it might be well to tell you of some of the customs and beliefs of the country of Lilliput. In this country, if a person is accused of a crime and is proved innocent, the accuser is put to death. Here, they look upon fraud as a greater crime than stealing. They say that care may keep a person's belongings from being stolen, but honesty has no protection against lies.

Whoever can bring proof that he has obeyed the laws of the country for seventy-three moons is given by the government a sum of money and the title of *Snilpail*, or Legal. The people thought it a terrible mistake when I told them that those who broke our laws in Europe were punished but those who kept them were not rewarded.

In government, they care more for good morals than great abilities. They believe that power can never be put in more dangerous hands than those of a man who is evil and has great abilities to carry out his evil.

Being ungrateful is a great crime. If a man is bad to one who has been good to him, they believe, he will be even worse to those who have done him no service. And therefore such a man is not fit to live.

Their thoughts about the duties of parents and children are very different from ours. Since men and women come together because of nature, they do not believe that a child owes anything to his parents for bringing him into the world. The young ladies are taught to be as much ashamed of being cowards and fools as the men. And I saw no difference in their education.

Before I tell of my leaving this kingdom, I should tell of the plot which had for two months been forming against me. I learned of it in this way. While I was getting myself ready to visit the island of Blefuscu, a person high in the court of Lilliput came to me very privately at night. I had once done him a great favor, and he had come to repay me.

"You know," he said, "that the High Admiral has been your enemy ever since you captured the Blefuscu fleet, in which he saw his glory dimmed. In private meeting of the Council, he and the Empress have accused you of treason. You are accused of making water in the area of the palace. This is your first and greatest crime. You are accused of refusing to help his Imperial Majesty destroy the empire of Blefuscu and of making friends of the Blefuscudians. And you are accused of wanting to go to Blefuscu.

"Because of these crimes, the Admiral and his friends say that you must be put to a terrible death. Reldresal, who is the Emperor's chief adviser, says that killing you would make the king look ungrateful after all that you have done for him. He suggests that your eyes should be put out. There had been much talk of what to do with your body if you were killed, and it was that, I think, that decided the case. Three days from now you will lose your eyes.

"I leave it to you what you will do. I must go now as secretly as I came."

After he left, I remained alone with my doubts and my confusions. It was a custom in that country that, when the court had decided on some cruel punishment, the Emperor always made a speech saying that his great mercy was well known through the world. Nothing so frightened the people as to hear about his Majesty's mercy. The more his mercy was praised, the crueler the punishment would be. For myself, I am such a bad judge of these things that I could not see the mercy in my sentence.

I decided to flee the country.

The next day, I put my clothes into a battleship to keep them dry and, pulling it behind me, I waded and swam to Blefuscu. There I was welcomed.

21

CHAPTER FOUR

Three days after I arrived in Blefuscu, a most lucky accident happened. I saw, at a distance in the sea, something that looked like a boat overturned. Wading closer to it, I saw that it was indeed a real boat. It had been driven, I guessed, from a ship by a storm.

I went at once to his Imperial Majesty and asked him to lend me twenty of his tallest ships and three thousand seamen. With their help I brought the boat near to shore, turned it over, and saw that it was not much hurt.

Five hundred workmen made two sails for my boat. I cut down some of their tallest trees for oars and masts. The Emperor then filled my boat with food and gave me some live cattle to take back with me. And I set off for home.

I was two days gone when I saw a sail in the distance. As I came up to it, my heart leaped in me to see her English flag. The captain was a kind man and a good sailor. At first, when I told my story, he thought that the dangers I had been through had disturbed my mind. But then I showed him the cattle and he was much amazed.

Back in England, I made a large sum of money showing the cattle to curious people. I stayed only two months with my wife and family and then set off again.

The Voyage to Brobdingnag
CHAPTER ONE

Two months after my return from Lilliput, I again left my native country, in the *Adventure*, bound for Surat. A little to the east of the Molucca Islands, a southern storm began to set in. During this storm, we were carried a great distance to the east, so that the oldest sailor on board could not tell in what part of the world we were.

On the 17th of June, 1703, we came into view of a great island or continent. Our captain sent a dozen of his men in a boat ashore to find fresh water. I went with them, to see the country and make what discoveries I could.

When we came to land, our men set out to find water near the sea, and I walked alone about a mile into the land. The land I saw was dry and rocky. Seeing nothing of interest, I returned towards the sea. There, I saw our men already in the boat and rowing for dear life to the ship. I was going to call after them, when I saw a huge creature walking after them into the sea! He waded not much deeper than his knees and took huge steps. But our men had a head start and the monster was not able to catch the boat.

I ran as fast as I could the way I first went and then climbed up a steep hill. As I came over the hill, I had a view of the country. The first thing that surprised me was the length of the grass, which was about twenty feet high!

I found a highway (for that is what I thought it was, although it served the people there only as a footpath through a field of barley). I came to a stile to pass from this field into the next. It was impossible for me to climb

this stile, however, because every step was six foot high.

I was trying to find some hole in the fence when I saw one of the people of the land coming towards the stile. He seemed about as tall as an ordinary church steeple. He took about ten yards at every step. I was struck with fear and amazement and ran to hide myself in the corn.

Scared as I was, I could not help thinking of Lilliput, where I was able to pull an Imperial Fleet in my hand. Philosophers are right when they tell us that nothing is great or little except by comparison.

Suddenly, I realized that the monster was about to squash me to death under his foot, and I screamed as loud as fear could make me. At that, the huge man stopped and looked around him and at last spied me on the ground. He reached down and took me up between his finger and his thumb and brought me within three yards of his eyes.

I decided not to struggle, but placed my hands together as though to pray and spoke in a humble way. He seemed pleased with this and began to look at me with interest. Then he ran along with me to his master, who was a farmer.

The farmer placed me softly on the ground on all fours. I got immediately up and walked to let these people know that I was not going to run away. I pulled off my hat and made a low bow. After a time, the farmer decided I was a thinking creature. Then he took his handkerchief out of his pocket, doubled it, and spread it on his hand, which he placed flat on the ground with the palm upwards. He made a sign for me to step onto it, which I could easily do as it was not more than a foot in thickness.

In this way, he carried me to his house. He called his wife and showed me to her. But she screamed and ran back as at the sight of a toad or spider. However, when she had seen for a while how I acted, she began to like me.

It was about twelve at noon, and a servant brought in dinner in a dish about four-and-twenty foot across. The wife cut up a bit of meat and placed it in front of me. She sent her maid for a thimble, which held about two gallons, and filled it with drink. I took up the cup with much difficulty in both hands and made a toast. This made my master (as I shall now call him) laugh loudly.

In the middle of dinner, my mistress's cat jumped into her lap. It seemed to be three times larger than an ox and looked very fierce. But there was no danger. The cat took not the least notice of me.

My mistress had a daughter of nine years old. Her mother and she fixed up her doll's bed for me. This was my bed all the time I stayed with those people. This young girl made me seven shirts of cloth as fine as she could get, which was rougher than burlap. She washed them for me with her own hands. She also taught me the language. She was very nice and not more than forty foot high, being little for her age. She gave me the name of *Grildrig*, which meant "little man." I called her *Glumdalclitch*, or "little nurse."

It now began to be known and talked of in the neighborhood that my master had found a strange animal in the field. Another farmer who lived near by came on a visit. I was immediately brought out and put on the table. I walked, drew my sword, asked the guest (in his own langauge) how he was, and told him he was welcome. After seeing this, he told my master he should show me as a sight on market day in the next town.

The next morning Glumdalclitch, my little nurse, told me the whole thing. The poor girl cried with shame for what her father was going to do. She was afraid something would happen to me. For my own part, I was less worried. I had a strong hope that I should one day get back my liberty.

My master carried me in a box, with a few holes to let in air, the next market day to the town. He took along with him his little daughter. My master stopped at an inn and let the town know of a strange creature to be seen at the Sign of the Green Eagle.

I was placed upon a table in the largest room of the inn. My master, for safety's sake, allowed only thirty

people at a time to see me. I walked about the table as Glumdalclitch told me to. She asked me questions, and I answered them, in their language and as loud as I could. I drew my sword and waved it in the air in the manner of fencers in England. I was that day shown to twelve sets of people. At the end of the day I was tired half to death.

My master, finding how much money he could make from me, decided to take me to the largest cities in the kingdom. With Glumdalclitch, we set out in a carriage. We were ten weeks on our trip, and I was shown in eighteen large towns, besides many villages and private homes. Finally we reached the capital city. My master rented a large room and a large table upon which I acted my part. I was shown ten times a day to the wonder of all people.

Soon, I began to be sick from the hard work and long hours. The more money my master made, the more he wanted. I was reduced almost to a skeleton. Then a gentleman came from the court of the king. He told my master to take me to the court to entertain the queen and her ladies.

Her Majesty was delighted with me. She asked me questions about my country and my travels, which I answered as clearly as I could. She asked whether I would like to live at Court. I answered that I should be proud to spend my life in Her Majesty's service.

My master knew how sick I was and did not believe I would last another month, so he agreed to sell me and demanded, and got, a thousand pieces of gold. I then begged the queen to hire Glumdalclitch, who took care of me with so much kindess. Her Majesty agreed. The farmer was happy to have his daughter at Court, and the poor girl herself was not able to hide her joy.

Then the queen carried me to the king. He was as wise as any person in his kingdom, but when he saw me, he decided that I was a wind-up toy, made by some very clever artist. But when he heard me speak, and heard that what I said made sense, he could not hide his amazement.

His Majesty sent for three scientists. These gentlemen looked me over and agreed that I could not have been made according to the regular laws of nature. I was clearly not able to keep myself alive! I was not fast. I could not climb trees or dig holes in the earth. All other animals, except snails and insects, were too large for me to eat.

They decided I was a freak of nature. Modern scientists have invented this wonderful solution to all difficult problems. Before, the stupid and foolish old scientists had to say it was magic. I told the king that I came from a country where there were millions of people my size. And there, I could defend myself and find food as well as any of his people. The scientists only smiled.

The king sent away his wise men and told the queen to take care of me. The queen told her carpenter to make a box that would be my bedroom. The queen also ordered the thinnest silks that could be found to make me clothes. They were not much thicker than an English blanket.

In the time that followed, I learned about the country that it is about six thousand miles in length and from three to five wide. I believe that our scientists in Europe have made a mistake in thinking that there is nothing but sea between Japan and California. The kingdom is bordered on one side by mountains thirty miles high, with volcanoes on the top. On the other three sides, there is ocean. But there is not one seaport in the whole kingdom. These people are completely cut off from the rest of the world.

I should have lived happily enough here if my littleness had not caused several ridiculous and troublesome accidents. Glumdalclitch often carried me into the gardens of the palace in my small box and would sometimes take me out of it and hold me in her hand or set me down to walk. One day, she left me on a smooth piece of grass and went for a walk with her teacher. Suddenly there fell a terrible shower of hail. I was immediately struck to the ground. I managed to creep under a plant, but I was so bruised that I could not leave my room for ten days.

A more dangerous accident happened to me in the same garden. Again my little nurse had left me alone, thinking I was safe. While she was gone, a small white dog that belonged to one of the gardeners happened to come near where I was. He took me in his mouth, and ran straight to his master, wagging his tail. It was my good luck that he was so well trained that he carried me without hurting me. The poor gardener took me to my little nurse, who had come back to where she left me. This accident made her decide never to let me out of her sight again.

CHAPTER TWO

The king questioned me closely about my own country.

He asked me about our government, our schools, our law courts. I told him of our history. He was amazed to hear of so many wars. We must be very bad people or have very bad neighbors. He was even more amazed to hear of an army that existed in peacetime.

Finally, he said, "My little friend, you have spoken well of your country. You have proven that ignorance, laziness, and dishonesty are the proper qualities of a lawmaker. You have shown that your lawyers are the people who are best at getting around the law. From all you have said, there is no time when virtue is necessary for getting any job or office, no time when priests are promoted in the church because of their goodness or learning. In your country, soldiers are not rewarded for their bravery, senators for their love of their country, or judges for their fairness and wisdom.

"You have spent much of your life in traveling, so I can only hope that you have escaped the wickedness of your country. For the rest, I can only believe that most of your people are the most evil race of disgusting little rats that nature ever allowed to crawl on the face of the earth."

If I did not love the truth so much, I would hide this

part of my story. I am as sorry as my readers can be that such words were spoken about my country. I can only defend myself by saying that I did not answer all his questions honestly. I made everything about our country seem better than it was.

But you should forgive the king. He lives so apart from the world that he does not understand it. Let me give you an example. This will be difficult to believe, but it is true. One day, I told His Majesty about gunpowder and how it was used in our country. I said that it would drive a ball of iron or lead so hard that nothing would be able to stand up against its force. I said that it could destroy large parts of an army, that it could batter the strongest walls to the ground. I explained that it would rip up pavements, tear houses to pieces, and dash the brains of all who came near. I then said that I knew how to make it and would teach His Majesty so that he could destroy any city in his kingdom that did not do exactly as he wished.

If you can believe it, the king was struck with horror! He was amazed that such a little insect as I could have such cruel ideas and that I could speak with so little feeling about all these scenes of blood and destruction. He said that, while few things made him so happy as new knowledge, he would rather lose half his kingdom than know the secret of gunpowder. He ordered me, if I wanted to stay alive, never to talk of it again.

You see what happens when people know little of the world? Here was a king who had every quality that makes people love and admire their ruler — wisdom, learning, courage. And because of some foolish idea of kindness that we would not even think of in Europe, he let slip a chance to become the complete master of the lives, liberties, and fortunes of his people.

I believe the problem is that this country has not yet turned politics into a science. His Majesty often said that he hated all plotting and hiding in government. He did not know what I meant by a *secret of state*, if there was no enemy country in the case. His beliefs about government

were so narrow that he thought it required only common sense, justice, and mercy. And he said that whoever could make two ears of corn or two blades of grass to grow upon a spot of ground where only one grew before would do more service to his country than the whole race of politicians put together. Seeing his ignorance, I hope that the reader will forgive his words about our country.

CHAPTER THREE

All this time, I thought about my liberty. I was treated with much kindness. I was the favorite of the great king and queen and the delight of the whole court. But it was in a way that was not dignified for a human being. Also, I could not forget my family, and I wanted to be with people I could talk to as an equal. I wanted to walk about the streets and fields without fear of being stepped on by a frog or a young puppy.

About the beginning of my third year here, Glumdalclitch and I went with the king and queen to spend a few days at a palace near the seaside. I was carried in a very comfortable room about twelve foot wide, with a ring on top for a handle. Glumdalclitch and I were very tired, and she was so sick she had to stay in her room. I asked to go near the sea with a page. Glumdalclitch did not want to let me go. She burst into tears, as though she knew what was about to happen.

The boy took me out towards the rocks on the seashore and set me down. I soon fell asleep. I can only imagine that the page, thinking no danger could happen, went among the rocks to look for birds' eggs. However it happened, I found myself suddenly awaked with a violent pull on the ring on top of my box. I felt my box raised high in the air. Some eagle had got the ring of my box in his beak. He was going to let it fall on a rock, like a turtle in a shell, and then pick my body out and eat it.

All of a sudden, I felt myself falling down with amazing speed. My fall was stopped by a terrible squash that sounded louder than the falls of Niagara. I had fallen into the sea.

My box floated, but I expected every moment to see it dashed in pieces. A break in the glass would have been immediate death. But, even if I escaped these dangers, what could I hope for but a death of cold and hunger?

Suddenly, I heard, or at least thought I heard, some kind of scraping noise. I managed to move one of my chairs under the hole in the top of the box. I climbed up, and putting my mouth as near as I could to the hole, I called for help in a loud voice, in all the languages I knew. I now heard a trampling over my head, and somebody called through the hole with a loud voice, "If there be anybody below, let them speak." I answered.

I had been found by an English ship. From there I was taken, very weak, into the ship. The sailors were amazed and asked me a thousand questions. I was just as amazed at the sight of so many pygmies! That's what they looked like to me, because my eyes were so used to the monsters I had left.

The captain let me off when we neared my own town in England. When I came to my house, my wife ran out to hug me. But I stooped lower than her knees, thinking she would never be able to reach my mouth. I looked down upon the servants and one or two friends in the house as though they were pygmies. In a little time, my family and friends and I came to a right understanding. But my wife said that I should never go to sea anymore.

A Voyage to the Country of the Houyhnhnms
CHAPTER ONE

I stayed at home with my wife and children about five months very happily — if I could have learned the lesson of knowing when I was well. Then I accepted an offer to be captain of the *Adventure*.

I had several men grow ill and die, so that I was forced to take on more crew out of Barbados. I found afterwards that most of them had been pirates. They corrupted my other men and they all formed a plot to take the ship. They forced me into the longboat, letting me put on my best suit of clothes. And they were so kind as not to search my pockets, into which I had put what money I had and a few other things. At the first place where they discovered land, they set me down on the shore.

In this sad state, I went forward. Soon, I found a beaten road where I saw many tracks of human feet, and some of cows, but most of horses. At last I saw several animals in a field. Their shape was very strange and deformed. I lay down behind a bush to watch them better.

Their heads and chests were covered with a thick hair. They had beards like goats. They had hair on the fore-parts of their legs and feet, but the rest of their bodies were bare, so that I might see their skins, which were of a light brown color. They often stood on their hind feet. The females were not so large as the males. On the whole, I never saw in all my travels such a disagreeable animal.

Thinking that I had seen enough, I got up and went back to the road. I had not got far when I met one of these creatures on the road. The ugly monster stared at me as at an object he had never seen before. Then he lifted up his forepaw, whether out of curiosity or because he meant me harm, I could not tell. But I gave him a good blow with the flat side of my sword. I dared not strike him with the sharp edge for fear the people of the country might be angry if they discovered I had hurt any of their cattle.

When the beast felt the blow, he drew back and roared so loud that a herd of at least forty came flocking about me from the next field, howling. Suddenly, though, they all ran away. Looking on my left hand, I saw a horse walking softly in the field. The beasts had seen him first, and he was the cause of their flight.

The horse started a little when he came near me, then he looked at me with wonder. He looked at my hands and feet, walking around me several times. At last I reached out my hand towards his neck to stroke it. But he shook his head and bent his brows, softly raising up his right forefoot to remove my hand.

At about this time, another horse came up. The two horses gently struck each other's right hoof before neighing several times. They varied the sound, making it seem almost like speech. Then they turned to me again. The gray horse rubbed my hat with his right forehoof, knocking it nearly off my head. I took it off and put it back straight, and the horses seemed very surprised.

On the whole, these animals acted so reasonable and so clever that I decided they must be magicians who had taken the shape of horses. Thinking this, I said, "Gentlemen, if you are wizards, you can understand any language. Therefore, let me tell you I am a poor Englishman whose bad luck has brought him to your coast. I beg you to let me ride one of you, as if he were a real horse, to somewhere I can find food and shelter."

The two horses stood silent while I spoke. When I had ended, they neighed frequently towards each other. I saw that their language was very expressive. I had no idea what they were saying, but I could often hear the word *Yahoo*. As soon as they were silent, I said it boldly, imitating the neighing of a horse.

They were both very much surprised, and the brown horse tried me with a second word. It was much harder to say. In English, it might be spelled *Houyhnhnm.* It took me several tries to get it right, but I succeeded, and the horses were again amazed.

After some further conversation between them, the two friends again struck each other's hooves and parted. The gray horse made me signs that I should walk with him.

CHAPTER TWO

Having traveled about three miles, we came to a long kind of building. It was a large room with a smooth clay floor, and a manger along the whole length on one side. There were three horses and two mares, not eating, but some of them sitting up, which I very much wondered at.

There was a very pretty mare, with a colt and foal, sitting upon mats of straw.

The mare came up close to me. She looked at me carefully and then gave me a most scornful look. She turned back to the gray horse and I heard the word *Yahoo* repeated between them. I still did not know what it meant, but I soon learned, to my everlasting embarrassment.

The gray horse and his servant, a sorrel nag, led me out into a kind of court where there was another building. I saw three of those awful creatures I had met right after landing. They were feeding on roots and the flesh of some animals. And they were all tied by the neck to a beam. One of the beasts and I were brought close together and our faces carefully compared, both by the gray horse and by his servant, who then repeated several times the word *Yahoo.* To my horror and amazement, I suddenly saw in this disgusting animal a perfect human figure!

Next, the sorrel nag offered me a root. I took it in my hand and, having smelled it, returned it to him as nicely as I could. He gave me a piece of donkey's flesh, but I turned away from it in disgust. He showed me hay and oats, but I shook my head to show that neither of these were food for me. The horses showed great concern that I had nothing to eat. Finally, I roasted oats and ground them into flour. This flour I mixed with water to make a kind of cake, which I toasted at the fire and ate with milk.

I slept in a place separate from both the horses and the Yahoos.

My first task was to learn the language, which my master and his family were happy to teach me. In about ten weeks I was able to understand most of his questions. In three months I could give him some fairly good answers.

He was very curious to know from what part of the country I came. I answered that I came from over the sea, with many others of my own kind, in a great hollow vessel made from the bodies of trees. He said that I must be mistaken or that I *said the thing which was not*. (For they have no word in their language to express lying or falsehood.) He knew that it was impossible that a group of dumb animals could move a wooden vessel wherever they pleased upon the water. He asked me who made the ship and how it was possible that the Houyhnhnms of my country would leave it to the management of beasts.

I told him that the ship was made by creatures like myself who, in all the countries I had travelled, were the only governing, reasonable animals. And I said that, on arriving here, I was as much amazed to see the Houyhnhnms act like reasonable beings as he and his friends could be in finding some marks of thought in a creature he was please to call a Yahoo.

My master looked uneasy because *doubting* or *not believing* are so little known in this country that he did not know how to behave. I remember once we talked about *lying*. He had great difficulty understanding what I meant. The purpose of speech, he said, was to make us understand one another. Now, if any one *said the thing that was not*, that purpose was defeated. And this was all he could think about *lying*, which is so perfectly well understood and so universally practiced among human creatures.

But to return to the point, when I said that Yahoos governed my country, my master wanted to know whether we had Houyhnhnms among us and what they did. I said that we did and that they were called horses. I said that they were beautiful creatures, that they were strong and swift and, when they were owned by kind and wealthy people, they were treated with much care. But most horses belonged to people who made them work very hard and fed them badly. I explained about bridles and saddles and spurs, whips and harnesses and carriages.

My master was outraged and he wondered how we dared to get upon a Houyhnhnm's back. He was sure the weakest servant in his house would be able to shake off the strongest Yahoo or, by lying down and rolling upon his back, squeeze the beast to death.

I answered that our horses were trained up from a very early age to serve us. I said that they were severely beaten when they were young for not obeying. Also, if one misbehaved too often, it was used to pull plows and carriages. It is impossible to express my master's noble anger at our savage treatment of the Houyhnhnm race.

When we left that subject, my master asked to hear my own story. As I told him of hiring sailors in a foreign port, he stopped me. He asked me how I could persuade strangers from a different country to come with me. I explained that they were mostly criminals who had been forced to leave their places of birth.

I then had to explain what a criminal was.

It was with some difficulty that I tried to explain gambling and drinking, murder, theft, and forgery. He was completely at a loss to know what could be the reason for doing these things. To clear that up, I tried to give some idea of the desire for power and riches, of the terrible effects of anger and envy. After which, like one whose imagination was struck with something never seen or heard of before, he would lift up his eyes with amazement.

Another day, I attempted to explain war.

Having finally made him understand that the people in my country would come together to kill one another in large numbers on bloody battlefields, I was left with trying to explain why. Sometimes, I said, one prince went to war with another for fear the other should go to war with him. Sometimes, a war is entered upon because the enemy is too *strong*, and sometimes because he is too *weak*. Sometimes our neighbors *want* the *things* which we *have* or *have* the things which we *want*. And we fight till they take ours or give us theirs. We often make war against a country that is on our side if one of its towns is convenient for us. The trade of *soldier* is held the most honourable of all others, because the soldier is a Yahoo hired to kill in cold blood as many of his own species, who have never harmed him, as possibly he can.

"It is happy," my master said, "that your shame is greater than your danger and that nature has made you so completely incapable of doing much harm. Your mouths are flat with your faces, so you can hardly bite each other very effectively. Your claws are so short they cannot do much damage. You have not strength or hooves. I think, when you tell me about those who have been killed in battle, you must have *said the thing which is not.*

I could not help shaking my head and smiling a little as I explained about cannons, muskets, pistols, bullets, powder, swords, bayonets, battles, sieges, retreats, attacks, sea fights, ships sunk with a thousand men, twenty thousand killed on each side, dying groans, limbs flying in air, smoke, noise, confusion, fields covered with corpses left for food to dogs and wolves.

I would have gone on but my master commanded me to silence. He said he had heard too much upon the subject of war. He thought his ears, being used to such horrible words, might gradually hear them with less hatred.

To change the subject, I began to describe to him *money* and its uses. I said that when a Yahoo had a great store of this precious thing, he was able to buy whatever he wanted—the finest clothing, the noblest houses, the most expensive meats and drinks—and have his choice of the most beautiful females. Therefore, Yahoos thought they could never have enough money. The rich man, I explained, made money from the poor man's labour and there were a thousand of the poor for every one of the rich.

This my master did not understand at all. His confusion arose, I think, from his assumption that all animals had a right to their share in the productions of the earth.

From these conversations, and from my living three years in the country of the Houyhnhnms, I learned much of their habits and customs.

The Houyhnhnms have no idea of evil. Friendship and kindness are their greatest virtues. A stranger from the farthest part of the country is treated equally with the nearest neighbor and, wherever he goes, he looks upon himself as at home.

When a mare has had one foal of each sex, she and her husband have no more children. But she may bear a foal for another couple if they lose a child.

Children of both sexes are taught to work, exercise, and keep themselves clean. My master thought it monstrous that Europeans give the females a different kind of education from the males. By this arrangement, he said, one half of our natives are fit for nothing but bringing children into the world. And to trust the care of our children to such useless animals was yet a greater crime.

There is no continuing government among the Houyhnhnms. Every fourth year, there is a council of the whole nation. Here they talk about the condition of the different districts in the country. And if there is some problem, they see that it is attended to.

On the whole, life with these noble creatures was so filled with all that is fine and good and happy that I was satisfied to spend the rest of my days with them.

CHAPTER THREE

In the midst of all my happiness, and I when looked upon myself as fully settled for life, my master sent for me one morning. He told me that the last general assembly had seen much that was wrong in his keeping a Yahoo in his family more like a Houyhnhnm than a beast. The assembly did therefore *urge* him either to use me like the rest of the Yahoos or to order me to swim back to my home.

When I realized my master was sending me away, I was filled with horror. Even if were able, having no tools, to make a boat, I was unlikely to reach another country. And if I reached my home, how could I think without disgust of passing my days among Yahoos? I would not have the Houyhnhnms to show me virtue and nobility. But I knew that decisions of the assembly were based on solid reasons that would not be shaken by arguments of mine. So, with the sorrel nag, I spent two months building a boat.

On my journey home, I was picked up by a Portuguese ship. I was so sickened by being close to Yahoos that I tried to throw myself into the ocean, but I was prevented and, at last, I found my way home. At the time I am writing, it is five years since my return to England. I am still not able to bear the smell or touch of Yahoos, not even my wife and children. I spend my days in the stable with two horses who have become my dear friends.

GLOSSARY

barley   (bär′ lē) a cereal grass often used in breakfast foods and malt beverages

gunpowder   (gən′ paůd ər) an explosive powder that is used in charges in gunnery

hospitality   (häs pə tal′ ə tē) generous and cordial treatment

ignorance   (ig′ nə rəntz) the state of lacking knowledge or understanding of something

imperial   (im pir′ ē əl) relating to an empire

stile   (stīl) a stair or set of stairs used to get over a fence or wall

translation   (trans lā′ shən) the changing from one language to another

treason   (trēz′ ən) the crime of trying to overthrow a government

wizard   (wiz′ ərd) a person who is skilled in magic